Adam Raccoon
in
Lost Woods

Glen Keane

Chariot Books
DAVID C. COOK PUBLISHING CO.

To Claire

Chariot Books is an imprint of David C. Cook
Publishing Co.
David C. Cook Publishing Co., Elgin, Illinois 60120
David C. Cook Publishing Co., Weston, Ontario

ADAM RACCOON IN LOST WOODS
© 1987 by Glen Keane for text and illustrations

First printing, 1987
Printed in Singapore
92 91 90   5

Library of Congress Cataloging-in-Publication Data

Keane, Glen, 1954-.
  Adam Raccoon In Lost Woods.

  (Parables for kids)
  Summary: Adam Raccoon learns a lesson about caring
too much for material things.
  [1. Raccoons—Fiction. 2. Animals—Fiction. 3. Parables]
I. Title. II. Series: Keane, Glen, 1954-. Parables for kids.
PZ7.K2173Ae   1987   [E]   86-30951
ISBN 1-55513-088-7

The sun had not yet risen
in Master's Wood.

Nearly everyone was sleeping.
A single light shone from
Adam Raccoon's window.

He had been up for hours
getting ready for the big day!

KNOCK KNOCK
"That must be him!" Adam
said, running to open the door.

There stood the mighty lion,
King Aren.

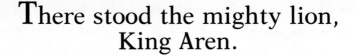

"Are you ready to go on the
hike, Adam? The sun is
almost up," he said.

"Yes! Wait one second. I'll be right back!" Adam replied.

"Okay, I'm ready!" Adam said.

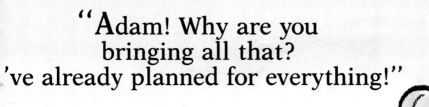

"Uh . . . Adam, you're
heading the wrong way.
Follow me."

And so they started on their journey.

Adam quickly realized this
was not going to be as easy
as he thought.

Stopping
at a stream,
King Aren said,
"Crossing this stream
is going to be tricky.
Watch how I do it, Adam."

Grabbing a hanging vine,
King Aren swung easily
across the stream.

But all Adam could see was
the stuff he was carrying.

Now it was Adam's turn.
Carefully he stretched his
foot to the first rock.

The rocks were very slippery.

Adam frantically grabbed
for his things as they floated
down the stream.

It was too late.
He was only able to save his
little red ball.

"Adam, try not to worry about losing your things. You really don't need them when you're with me," King Aren said.

"What about my ball? Can
I bring it? It's so small. . . .

And besides, it's the only
thing I have left."

"It will only cause you more trouble, Adam. Come on now. Stay close by my side," King Aren said.

LOST WOODS

Adam followed him, clutching his little red ball. Ahead of them lay the dangerous Lost Woods.

King Aren had traveled this
way many times before.

Holding tight to the king's
hand, Adam knew he would
be safe.

A howling sound swirled
around them.

It was the cold wind
whistling through the
twisted trees.

The Lost Woods had many twisted paths that crisscrossed here and there. But King Aren always knew which way to turn.

Soon the woods began to
brighten.
Flowers bloomed
everywhere.

Adam was feeling safer. He let go of the king's hand and started to play with his ball.

Whoops!
The ball rolled
off the path and into the woods,

Down the hill
nd through a log.

It rolled to a stop in a little clearing.
Adam picked it up and
turned to go back.

But which way was back?

Nothing looked familiar as
he headed in what he
thought was the right direction.

The woods seemed darker
and colder now. Frantically
Adam tried to find a way back.

"King Aren, I'm lost!"

Exhausted, Adam fell to the ground.
"It's hopeless. I'll never find
my way back," he said.

Then Adam realized he
wasn't alone.

GRRRRR

A low growling surrounded him.

Wolves!

From behind every tree and
rock crept a hungry wolf.
Adam tried to scream for help.

With one mighty roar the
wolves leaped at Adam.

Adam waited . . . but nothing happened.

He took a peek and could hardly believe what he saw!

All around him the wolves
were cowering, as though
they were afraid.

Adam didn't understand.

Then he felt the big, strong
paw resting on his shoulder.

"King Aren!" Adam cried.
"It was you who scared
them away!"

"Adam," the king said.
"Aren't you leaving
something behind?"

"Nothing that I need as long
as I'm with you!" Adam replied.
And they continued on their way.

D o you find yourself telling your children stories to help them understand things you want them to learn or remember? Maybe you find yourself remembering the point of a sermon because of the illustration used.

Telling stories to convey truth is not new. Jesus often taught in parables.

Why do we use parables to teach? Because we *remember* stories—and the truths they hold.

Adam Raccoon and King Aren illustrate truths from God's Word in language and experiences children readily understand. While stories like these are not a substitute for the Bible, they will enhance and reinforce the Bible teaching your children receive.

What does it mean to follow Jesus? *Adam Raccoon in Lost Woods* illustrates this as Adam learns (the hard way) that he can only follow King Aren when he is no longer distracted by his own "stuff."

Children need to understand there is nothing wrong with having things. But when the things—or activities—become more important to them than Jesus, problems arise. (As a follow-up to this story, read about the rich young ruler and Jesus in Luke 18:18-30.)

Discuss why Adam thought he needed all the things he took on the hike. Why did he get lost? Talk with your children about what's important to them and how these things can come between them and Jesus. Why did Adam leave his ball behind at the end of the story?

Another important aspect of following Jesus is His care for His children. Remind your children how He cares for them—just as King Aren protected Adam from the wolves.